Courtney Crumrin

Volume Seven

Tales of a Warlock

Courtney Crumrin

Volume Seven

Tales of a Warlock

Written & Illustrated by

Ted Naifeh

Colored by

Warren Wucinich

Original Series edited by

Jill Beaton

Collection edited by

Robin Herrera & Shawna Gore

Designed by

Keith Wood & Sonja Synak

Published by Oni-Lion Forge Publishing Group, LLC

Originally published as the Oni Press comics
Courtney Crumrin Tales: A Portrait of a Warlock as a Young Man and
Courtney Crumrin Tales: The League of Ordinary Gentlemen.

Courtney Crumrin, Volume 7, February 2021. Published by Oni-Lion Forge Publishing Group, LLC, 1319 SE Martin Luther King Jr. Blvd., Suite 240, Portland, OR 97214.

onipress.com lionforge.com
tednaifeh.com /tednaifeh

First Edition: February 2021

ISBN 978-1-62010-864-2
eISBN 978-1-62010-057-8

1 3 5 7 9 10 8 6 4 2

Library of Congress Control Number: 2020939322

Printed in China.

For Jill

Chapter One

WHO IS HE, PAPA?
THE NEW CLERK. HIRED HIM THIS MORNING.
WITHOUT TELLING ME?

ALICE, YOU MAY BE SURPRISED TO LEARN THAT I MAKE IMPORTANT DECISIONS IN THIS OFFICE DAILY WITHOUT CONSULTING YOU.

HE'S QUITE A BRIGHT LAD. YOU'LL GET ALONG FINE.
BUT WHY? DON'T YOU THINK I CAN MANAGE?

I RECALL YOU EXPRESSING AN INTEREST IN MY...

...OTHER WORK.

IT HAD BEEN A DREAM OF MINE FOR YEARS, TO HELP FATHER WITH THE SOCIETY.
OF COURSE, HE'D NEVER TAKEN MY INTEREST SERIOUSLY. HE THOUGHT I WAS JUST A SILLY GIRL WITH ROMANTIC NOTIONS.

HORACE W. CRISP
ATTORNEY AT LAW
BUT I KNEW HOW TO GET PAST SUCH PREJUDICES. THE SECRET IS TO NEVER BACK DOWN, AND NEVER GIVE UP.

RATHER LIKE COURTING A YOUNG LADY, I SUPPOSE.
MISS CRISP?
YES?
WOULD YOU LIKE... THAT IS, I WAS WONDERING...

I THOUGHT IT MIGHT BE BEST IF I WALKED YOU HOME.
DID YOU?

TO BE QUITE HONEST, I'D LIKED ALOYSIUS FROM THE FIRST.
HE WAS POLITE WITHOUT BEING OVERLY FRIENDLY AND DIDN'T ASSUME HE WAS SMARTER THAN I WAS—A RARE COURTESY AMONG MEN HIS AGE.

THOUGH THIS WAS A BIT OF A SHOCK.
I'M QUITE CAPABLE OF WALKING MYSELF HOME, THANK YOU.

I DO IT EVERY DAY, YOU SEE.

I BEG YOUR PARDON. WHAT I MEANT WAS-
WHAT'S THAT?

OH, THIS? I'M NOT SURE. I WAS GOING TO ASK YOU.

MULTIPLE VANISHINGS
THE SORCERER OF GREEN STREET
1912 SIGHTINGS OF THE HILLSBOROUGH BOGIE
THIS WAS MISFILED UNDER HILLSBOROUGH *PROPERTY* DISPUTES.

NEEDLESS TO *SAY*, I WAS RATHER TAKEN *ABACK* BY IT.

UNTIL RECENTLY, I'D SEEN ONLY GLIMPSES OF FATHER'S REAL WORK. I COULDN'T HELP BUT LINGER OVER THEM A MOMENT.
IS THIS SOME SORT OF *HOBBY* OF MR. CRISP'S? COLLECTING HUMBUG *STORIES*?

IT'S NONE OF YOUR *CONCERN*.
I MEANT NO *OFFENSE*.

BUT YOU MUST ADMIT, IT ALL SEEMS A BIT SILLY. ISN'T THAT LON CHANEY?

YOU DON'T KNOW WHAT YOU'RE TALKING ABOUT!
THWOKK

YOU DON'T SERIOUSLY BELIEVE ANY OF THAT NONSENSE? MY DEAR YOUNG LADY-

YOU WATCH YOUR TONE WITH ME, SIR.
I'M NOT YOUR DEAR ANYTHING.
SMAKK

MY APOLOGIES, MISS CRISP.

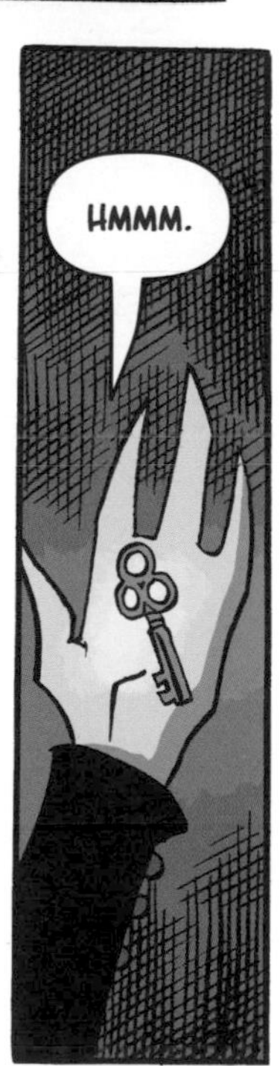
HMMM.

I KNEW I WAS ACTING FOOLISH.

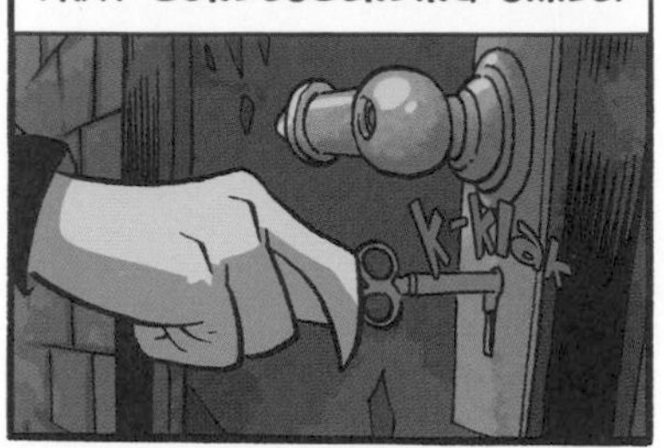
BUT I COULDN'T BEAR THE THOUGHT OF ALOYSIUS, DAY AFTER DAY, LOOKING AT ME WITH THAT CONDESCENDING SMILE.
K-KLAK

IF THERE'S ONE THING I CAN'T BEAR, IT'S BEING THOUGHT A FOOLISH FEMALE.
GOOD LORD! WHAT IS ALL THIS?
THE IRONY IS THAT THIS VERY PHOBIA DRIVES ME TO FOOLISH ACTS.

THE ANTI SORCERY SOCIETY
THE ANTI-SORCERY... THAT'S AN UNFORTUNATE TITLE.

I WOULDN'T SUGGEST ABBREVIATING IT.
I KNOW. THEY WERE CONSIDERING "THE LEAGUE OF ST. GEORGE," OR SOME SUCH THING, BUT FATHER WAS AGAINST ANYTHING SO MYSTICAL.
THEY'VE BEEN DEBATING A NEW NAME FOR MONTHS.

REALLY, MISS CRISP. I HAVE EVERY RESPECT FOR YOUR FATHER...
BUT THIS OFFENDS REASON.
#37 MAGIC WAND

OH? I WONDER WHAT LON CHANEY HAS TO SAY ABOUT IT.

WHAT ON EARTH IS THAT?

AIN'T IT OBVIOUS? I'M A SCORT-ISH TERRIER.
YEH DAFT BUGGER.

PRETTY GOOD MAKE-UP, EH?
WHO THE DEVIL LEFT THIS DOOR WIDE OPEN?

ALICE? WHAT IN HEAVEN'S NAME IS GOING ON?
THIS IS MY REWARD FOR TAKING YOU INTO MY CONFIDENCE?

WHAT IS HE DOING HERE?
I... I...

I FOUND THIS IN YOUR FILES, SIR.

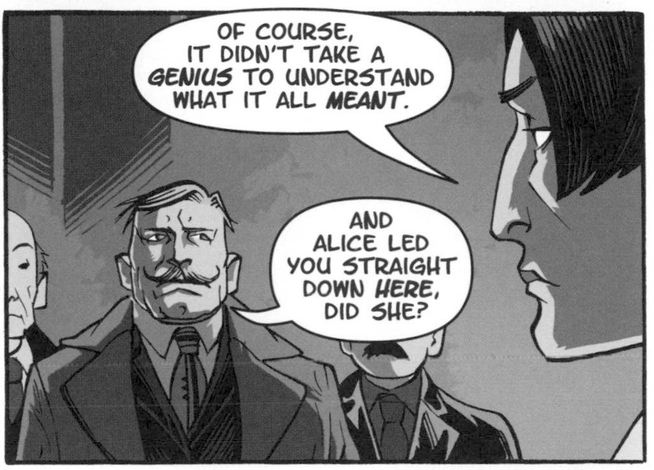
OF COURSE, IT DIDN'T TAKE A GENIUS TO UNDERSTAND WHAT IT ALL MEANT.
AND ALICE LED YOU STRAIGHT DOWN HERE, DID SHE?

I ONLY WANTED TO BE OF SOME SERVICE TO THE SOCIETY.
HIS SINCERITY WAS VERY... PERSUASIVE.

DON'T BE TOO HARD ON THEM, WILL. I'M SURE THEY MEAN WELL.
THAT'S NOT THE ISSUE.

SECRECY IS A FINE THING, WILL, BUT LOOK AT THIS MESS.

SOMEONE'S GOT TO DO THE HOUSEKEEPING.

WHY ARE YOU ANGRY?
I'M NOT ANGRY.
ALRIGHT, I'M ANGRY.

IF YOU WERE GOING TO ALTER THE TRUTH, WHY DIDN'T YOU JUST TELL FATHER THAT YOU FOUND THE PLACE BY ACCIDENT?

HE WOULDN'T HAVE BELIEVED THAT.
WHO KNOWS, HE MIGHT HAVE EVEN THOUGHT I WAS A... SPY OR SOMETHING.
I SUPPOSE.

IT'S JUST THAT IT TOOK ME YEARS TO GAIN HIS TRUST.

PERHAPS, BUT HE HARDLY HAD A CHOICE WITH ME.

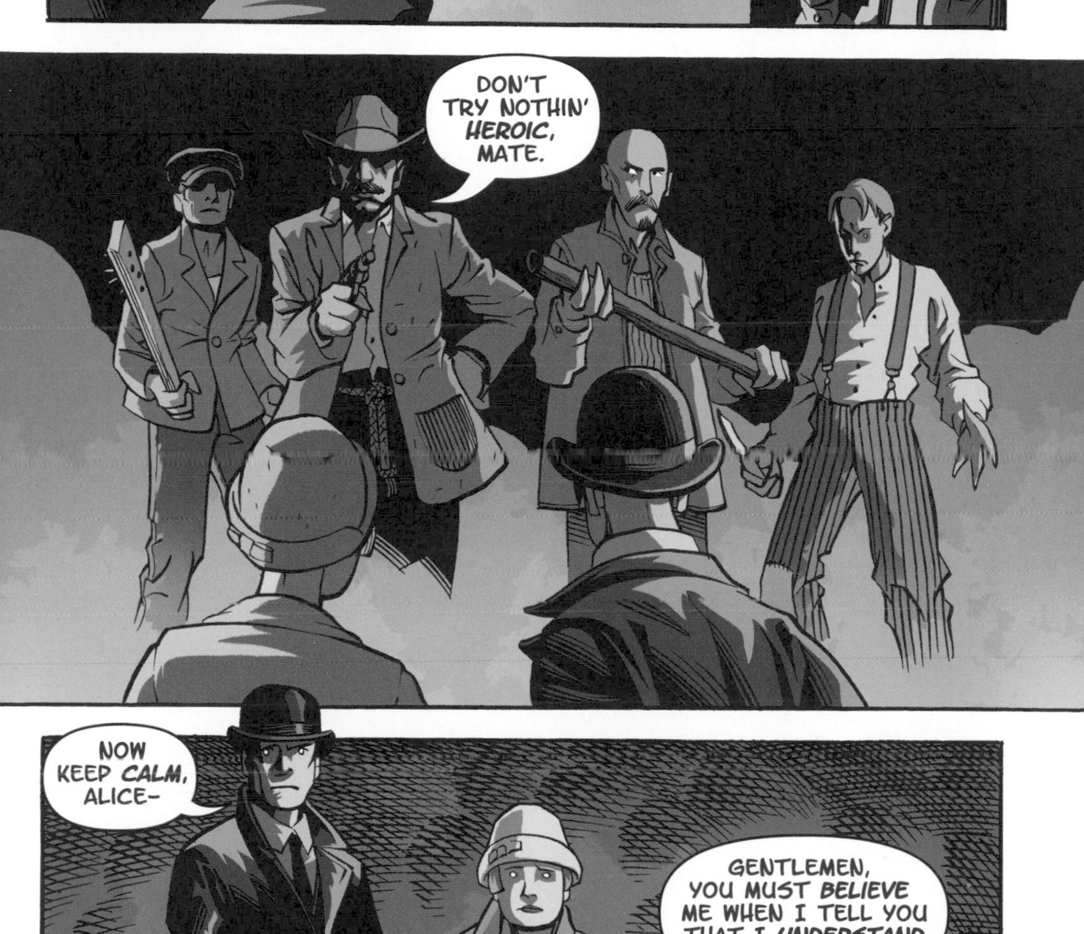
DON'T TRY NOTHIN' HEROIC, MATE.

NOW KEEP CALM, ALICE-
GENTLEMEN, YOU MUST BELIEVE ME WHEN I TELL YOU THAT I UNDERSTAND YOUR PLIGHT.

MY FATHER IS WILLIAM CRISP. I'M SURE YOU'VE HEARD OF HIM.
HE WORKS TIRELESSLY TO ALLEVIATE THE INEQUALITIES THAT REDUCE MEN SUCH AS YOURSELVES TO SUCH DESPERATE ACTS.

MMM-HMM.

MISS CRISP, WHILE I'M SURE THAT UNDER OTHER CIRCUM-STANCES THESE MEN MIGHT APPRECIATE YOUR WORDS...
I SUSPECT THAT JUST NOW THEY'D PREFER YOUR PURSE.

AND BY THE LOOKS OF THEM, THEY NEED IT MORE THAN YOU DO.
MUCH OBLIGED, MATE.

BUT IT'S NOT JUST MONEY WE WANT FROM HER...
FINE LOOKIN' LADY THAT SHE IS.

AH, I SEE.
THAT, I'M AFRAID, IS SOMETHING I CAN'T ALLOW.
WELL, WE HADN'T PLANNED ON ASKIN' YOUR LEAVE, MATE.

I NEVER THANKED YOU PROPERLY, MISS CRISP.
WHAT?

FOR YOUR TRUST IN MY DISCRETION.
I DON'T THINK NOW IS THE RIGHT-

I'VE ALREADY GIVEN YOU MY WORD TO KEEP YOUR SECRET.
WHAT ARE YOU-

I MUST NOW ASK THE SAME COURTESY OF YOU.
NOW?

YES.
ALRIGHT, BUT WHAT-

YOU SEE, THE FACT OF THE MATTER IS...

I AM A SORCERER MYSELF.

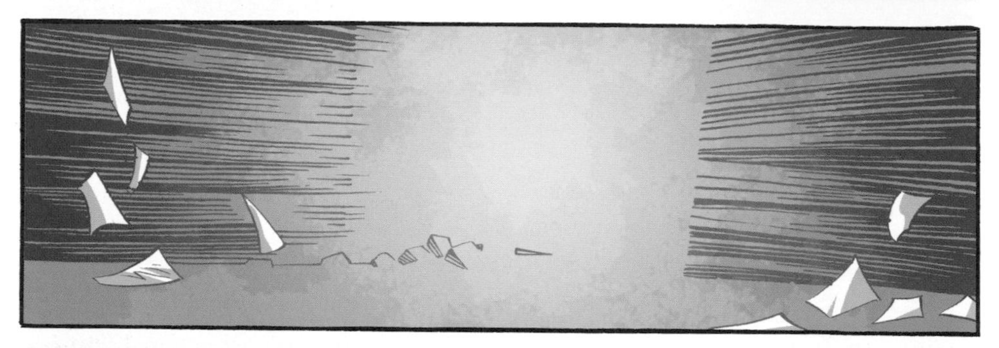

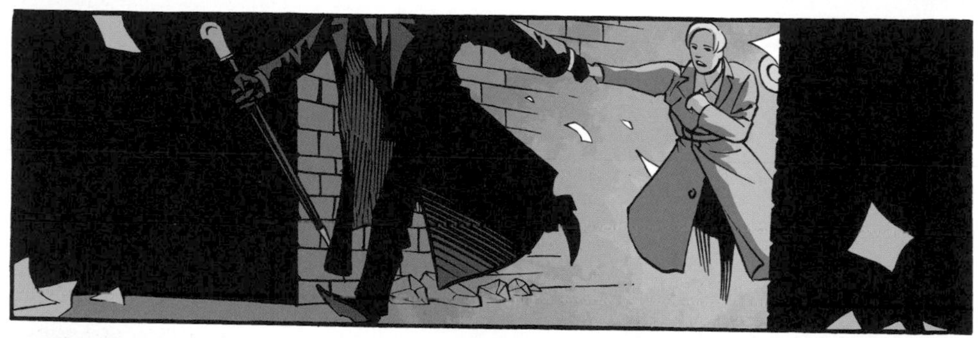

WHAT THE BLEEDIN' 'ELL WAS THAT?
I DON'T KNOW. WHAT HAPPENED TO ME CLOTHES?
LEAST YOU STILL GOT YOUR HAT. BETTER PUT IT TO USE THERE, LAD.

DAMNED KEY! C'MON, OPEN UP!

DON'T WORRY. I DON'T THINK THEY'RE IN ANY POSITION TO FOLLOW US.
I'M NOT RUNNING FROM THEM!

CALM YOURSELF, MADAM.

YOU'VE NOTHING TO FEAR FROM ME.

YOU STAY AWAY FROM ME!

AS YOU WISH. GOODNIGHT, MISS CRISP.

I'LL SEE YOU TOMORROW AT THE OFFICE.

I COULDN'T BELIEVE HE'D HAVE THE AUDACITY TO SIMPLY WALK INTO WORK AS THOUGH NOTHING WAS WRONG.
BUT HE WAS A BOLD ONE, ALRIGHT. AND SLIPPERY AS AN EEL.

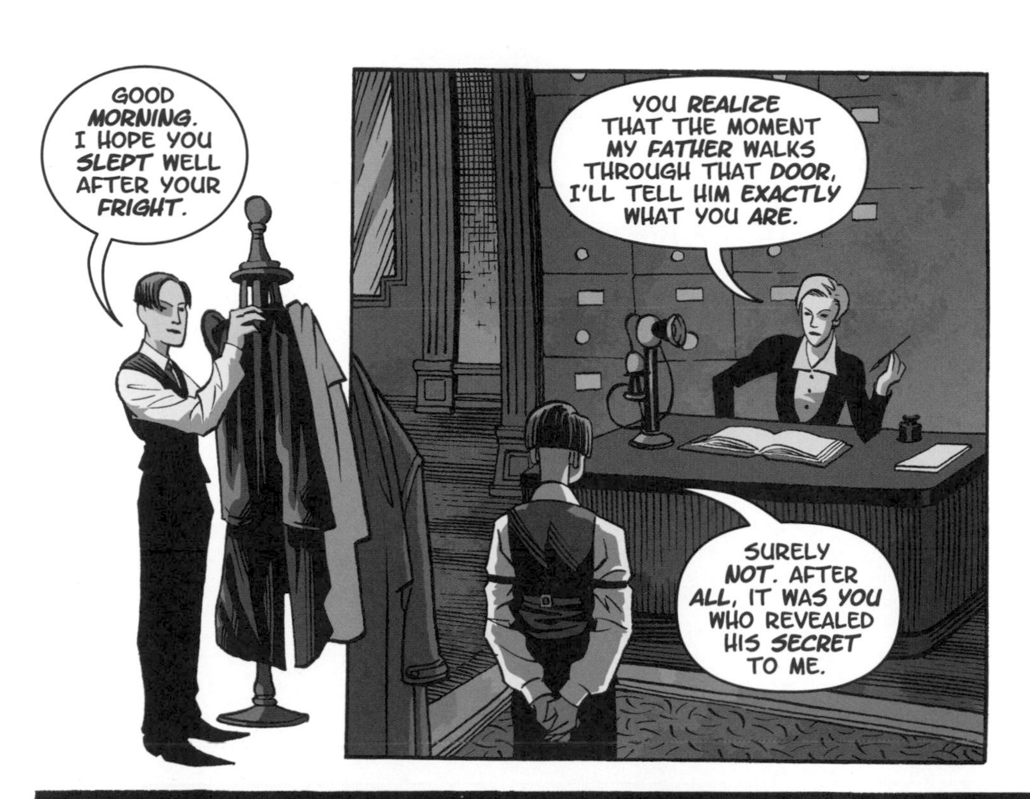
GOOD MORNING. I HOPE YOU SLEPT WELL AFTER YOUR FRIGHT.
YOU REALIZE THAT THE MOMENT MY FATHER WALKS THROUGH THAT DOOR, I'LL TELL HIM EXACTLY WHAT YOU ARE.
SURELY NOT. AFTER ALL, IT WAS YOU WHO REVEALED HIS SECRET TO ME.

IMAGINE HOW HE'LL REACT IF HE REALIZES YOU LED A WARLOCK INTO HIS SECRET HEADQUARTERS.
BESIDES, YOU WOULDN'T BREAK YOUR WORD, WOULD YOU?

ALICE. ALOYSIUS. DOWNSTAIRS, PLEASE.
NO LAW TODAY. WE HAVE MORE IMPORTANT BUSINESS.

ALICE, THIS IS GODFREY DANIELS.
HE'S AGREED TO BE OUR FIELD AGENT FOR THIS MISSION.
CALL ME GOOSE.
IT'S AN HONOR, SIR. I'VE READ ABOUT YOUR EXPLOITS IN THE GREAT WAR-
AH, ALOYSIUS. WOULD YOU BE SO KIND AS TO CLEAR UP THESE PAPERS?
GENTLEMEN!
OUR TARGET IS DR. ELKAN GUNZT.

I KNOW SOME OF YOU ARE FAMILIAR WITH HIS HISTORY. BUT FOR THOSE WHO AREN'T...

DR. GUNZT'S PUBLIC FACE IS THAT OF A RECLUSIVE BUT RESPECTED PHILANTHROPIST.
HE CAME TO MY ATTENTION FIVE YEARS AGO, WHEN HE DONATED FUNDS TO THE ST. IGNATIUS ORPHANAGE AND SAVED IT FROM BANKRUPTCY.
LITTLE DID I KNOW HIS REAL INTENTIONS.
WE LATER DISCOVERED THAT THIRTEEN CHILDREN HAVE BEEN TAKEN FROM THE ORPHANAGE TO HIS HOUSE...
NEVER TO BE SEEN AGAIN.
OUR INTELLIGENCE SUGGESTS HE'S BEEN USING THEM AS SACRIFICES IN COMPLEX MAGICAL RITUALS.

RECENTLY, DR. GUNZT HAS TAKEN AN INTEREST IN POLITICS.
WE BELIEVE THAT HIS BLACK MAGIC HAS INFLUENCED SEVERAL LOCAL ELECTIONS IN THE LAST TWO YEARS.
HE'S BUILDING POWER, GENTLEMEN. TO WHAT DARK PURPOSE, WE CAN ONLY SPECULATE.
Alexander DuMonde – 1909
Ralph Webster – after civil
Emerson
BUT JUDGING BY THE MEN HE'S PUT IN OFFICE, A PATTERN BEGINS TO FORM.
I'D ALWAYS BELIEVED THAT, AT LEAST IN THIS TOWN, YOU COULDN'T SIMPLY BUY YOUR WAY INTO ELECTED OFFICE.
NOT ANYMORE. THESE MEN TOGETHER OWN OVER HALF THE CITY.
AND EVEN THAT WASN'T ENOUGH. THEY WERE CHANGING THE LAWS SO THAT THEY COULD GRAB UP EVEN MORE.

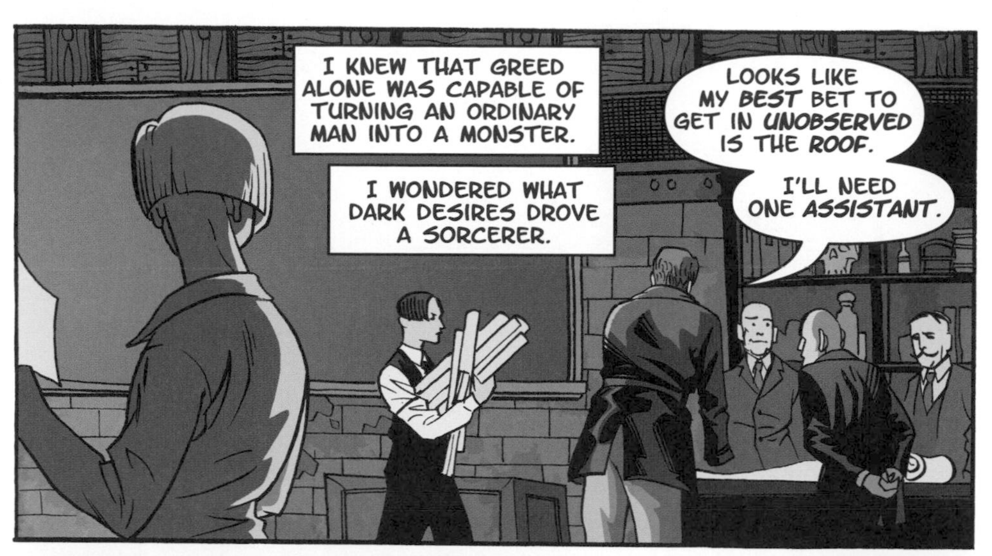
I KNEW THAT GREED ALONE WAS CAPABLE OF TURNING AN ORDINARY MAN INTO A MONSTER.
I WONDERED WHAT DARK DESIRES DROVE A SORCERER.
LOOKS LIKE MY BEST BET TO GET IN UNOBSERVED IS THE ROOF.
I'LL NEED ONE ASSISTANT.

WELL, TO BE SURE, YOU HAVE ANY OF US TO CHOOSE FROM, THOUGH, FRANKLY, I, BEING KNOWLEDGABLE IN-
NO, NONE OF YOU.

YOU GENTLEMEN COULDN'T HANDLE THE WALK UP THE GARDEN PATH WITHOUT A NAP AND A BRANDY AFTERWARDS.
OH, I SAY! HOLD ON!
THAT'S GOING A BIT FAR!

I'LL TAKE THE KID.
REALLY?

WAIT! WHAT ABOUT ME?

I HAVE FAR MORE EXPERIENCE IN THIS BUSINESS, AND I DARE SAY I'M PROBABLY IN BETTER SHAPE AS WELL.
YOU'VE GOT A POINT THERE.
NOT ON YOUR LIFE, YOUNG LADY.
I CAN'T TELL YOU WHAT AN HONOR IT IS TO BE WORKING WITH YOU, SIR.
GREAT.
HOPE YOU'RE UP TO IT, KID.
OOMPH!

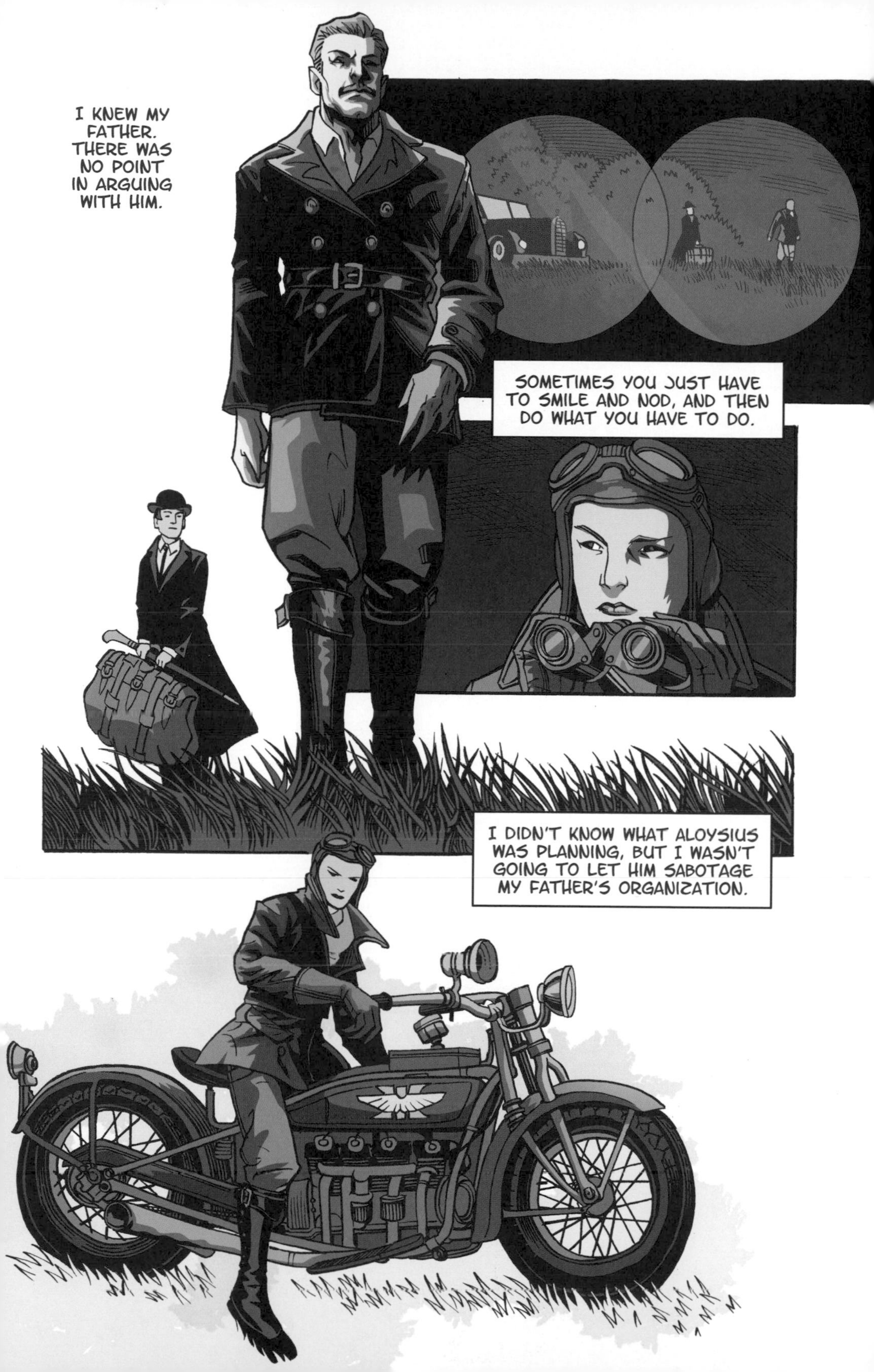
I KNEW MY FATHER. THERE WAS NO POINT IN ARGUING WITH HIM.
SOMETIMES YOU JUST HAVE TO SMILE AND NOD, AND THEN DO WHAT YOU HAVE TO DO.
I DIDN'T KNOW WHAT ALOYSIUS WAS PLANNING, BUT I WASN'T GOING TO LET HIM SABOTAGE MY FATHER'S ORGANIZATION.

thumph

JUST DROP THE BAG, KID. IT'S EASIER.

GOOD JOB.

LOOK OUT!
YOU'D THINK BALANCING THOSE HEAVY BOOKS WOULD HAVE GIVEN YOU MUSCLES.

HARRRROOPH!
WHOA, NELLIE!

THUNCH

HRAAACH!

K-SHINE!

HUR?

pakk
pakk

KRAKKK

THUMPH
OOF!

HRAAACH!
♫

MADE YOU LOOK.

Pakk

GOOD GRIEF, GIRL.
THIS ISN'T A FIELD TRIP.
LOOK, YOU NEED ME.
I JUST THOUGHT-

ALRIGHT. YOU HAD YOUR LITTLE ADVENTURE. NOW GO HOME LIKE A GOOD GIRL.
I CAN'T BABYSIT BOTH OF YOU.

JUNIOR HERE IS BAD ENOUGH.
THEN TAKE ME INSTEAD.

LISTEN, SISTER. SURE, YOU'RE TOUGH.
AND YEAH, YOU'RE A KNOCK-OUT.

BUT I NEED SOMEONE WHO CAN FOLLOW ORDERS.
GET ME?

DID YOU BRING ANYTHING TO DEFEND YOURSELF, BOY?
I'M NOT HELPLESS, SIR.

SEE?
HMPH.

MY POP HAD AN OLD SAYING.

"NEVER BRING A KNIFE TO A GUNFIGHT."

I'LL GET IN THROUGH THE ROOF AND UNLOCK A DOOR FOR YOU.
IF I GET A CHANCE.
WISE WORDS.

WHAT'S YOUR PLAN, WARLOCK?
SABOTAGE?

MR. DANIELS DOESN'T NEED A SABOTEUR.
HE'S DOING A GREAT JOB GETTING HIMSELF KILLED.
BUT HE'LL MAKE AN EXCELLENT DISTRACTION.

NO GUARDS ON THE ROOF. GOOD.

OI BEGS TO DIFFER.

GLASS WON'T BREAK, AND THERE'S A POWERFUL LOCKING SPELL.
THOSE CURTAINS LOOK NASTY, TOO.

TYPICAL, REALLY. ALL THIS COMPLEX, IMPRESSIVE MAGIC.
YET LIGHT CAN PASS RIGHT THROUGH.

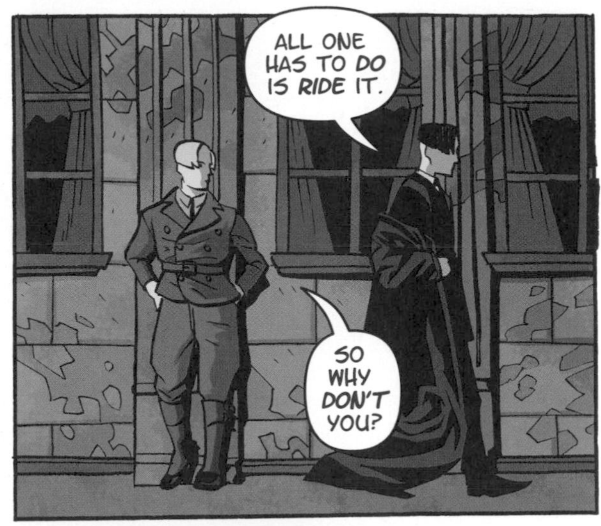
ALL ONE HAS TO DO IS RIDE IT.
SO WHY DON'T YOU?

DON'T THINK I WANT TO TANGLE WITH THOSE CURTAINS.

THEY DO LOOK A BIT DUSTY. SO WHAT-
KNOCK KNOCK
WANT TO SEE SOME WITCH-CRAFT?
CLOSE YOUR EYES AND LISTEN.
OKAY, SURE.

HEAR THE ECHO?
KNOCK KNOCK
YES.

IT'S GETTING FAINTER.
THAT'S WHAT IT SOUNDS LIKE ON THE OTHER SIDE.

OH MY!
A LOT EASIER THAN GOOSE'S WAY, I'LL WAGER.
SON OF A-!

EAT THIS, PAL!

KRASH

VULGAR, ISN'T IT? EXCESS IS SO UNBECOMING IN A WARLOCK.
RATHER LIKE A MONK WITH A ROLLS-ROYCE. STAY OFF THE CARPET, BY THE WAY.

ANOTHER POINTLESSLY ELABORATE PROTECTION SPELL.

MR. GUNZT SEEMS EAGER TO IMPRESS. I SUPPOSE SOME PEOPLE JUST PREFER THE HARD WAY.

WHAT THE DEVIL!?!

DAMN MAGIC!
I'M ALREADY SICK OF IT.
shinkk

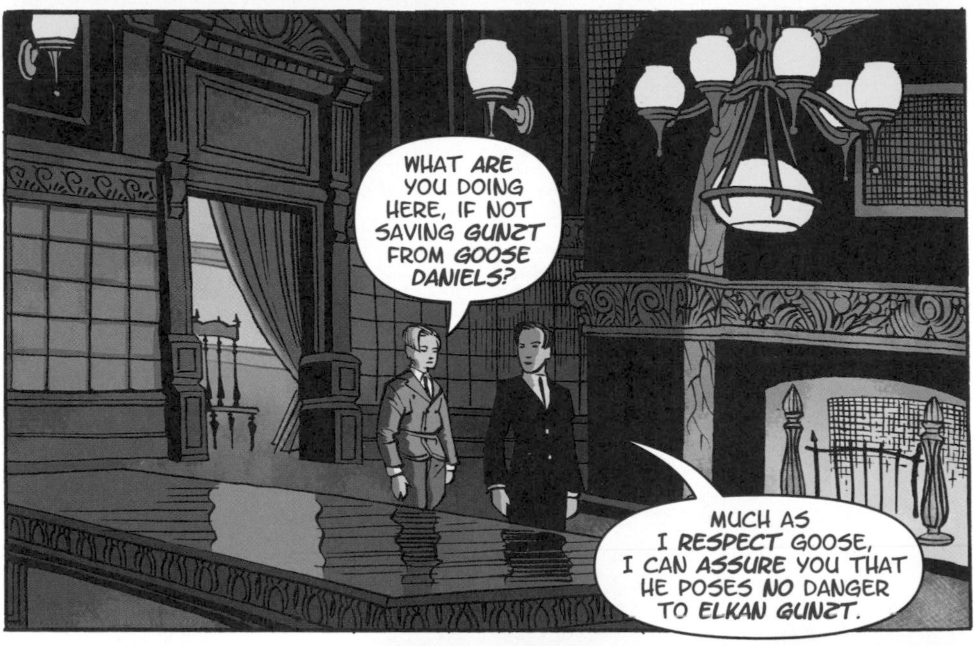
WHAT ARE YOU DOING HERE, IF NOT SAVING GUNZT FROM GOOSE DANIELS?
MUCH AS I RESPECT GOOSE, I CAN ASSURE YOU THAT HE POSES NO DANGER TO ELKAN GUNZT.

I HAVE... OTHER BUSINESS.
AH!

PERFECT.
WHAT ARE YOU DOING?

NO DOUBT GUNZT HAS CAST A LABYRINTH SPELL ON ALL THE DOORS AND STAIRCASES.

THEY'RE QUITE DIFFICULT TO PENETRATE.
WE'D BEST TAKE A ROUTE HE DOESN'T EXPECT.

OTHERWISE, WHO KNOWS WHERE WE MIGHT END UP.

WILL SOMEBODY TELL ME WHAT I'M DOING IN THE BASEMENT, WHEN ALL THE DAMNED STAIRCASES LED UP?
Bonch

YOUR FATHER IS QUITE CORRECT TO BELIEVE THAT SORCERERS EXIST THROUGHOUT THE WORLD.

AND IT'S TRUE THAT SOME OF THEM USE THEIR ARTS TO GAIN POWER OVER COMMON FOLK.

AND THOUGH HE MAY THINK THEM WICKED, HE'S NOT HALF SO OFFENDED AS THE MYSTICAL COMMUNITY.

TO INTERFERE IN ORDINARY SOCIETY IS FORBIDDEN BY ALL OF OUR LAWS.

YET, MOST MAGICAL FOLK DO LITTLE TO PREVENT IT, BEYOND SHUNNING THE OFFENDERS.

MEN LIKE GUNZT ARE EXILES FROM THEIR OWN PEOPLE.
ALAS, EXILE ONLY MAKES THEM WORSE, EVEN MORE LAWLESS AND CRUEL.

TRAGIC, REALLY.

KRASH

TOY SOLDIERS, HUH?
I KNOW THAT GAME.

ATTENNN-TION!
K-chunch

COMPANY...

FALL IN!
thwakkk

GUNZT!
GET YOUR BUTT OUT HERE!
I BEAT YOUR MAGIC!

YOU'VE THROWN EVERYTHING YOU'VE GOT AT ME, AND STILL I STAND!
COME OUT AND FACE ME LIKE A MAN, IF YOU'RE NOT A COWARD!

I BEG YOUR PARDON?
CAN I HELP YOU WITH SOMETHING?

YOU CAN PUT THOSE HANDS UP. YOU'RE COMING WITH ME.
AND YOU ARE?
GOOSE DANIELS.
NEVER HEARD OF HIM.
I'M JUST AN ORDINARY MAN, LIKE THE MEN YOU'VE USED YOUR UNGODLY POWERS TO CONTROL.
AND NOW YOU'RE GOING TO MEET THE JUSTICE OF ORDINARY MEN.
>YAWN<
FORGIVE ME, I'VE BEEN NAPPING. I DID WHAT NOW?

YOU'D... YOU WERE NAPPING?
THEN HOW...

OH, DEAR. HOW TIRESOME.
SNAP

I JUST DON'T UNDERSTAND ALL THIS POPULIST NONSENSE.
WHAT DO YOU SUPPOSE ORDINARY PEOPLE ARE FOR?
SQUAKKK
ARIEL!
OH, THERE YOU ARE.
CLEAN UP THIS MESS.

AND INFORM THE CHEF THAT DINNER TONIGHT WILL BE...
AHEM, GOOSE.

GULP.

IF YOU TWO MAKE YOURSELVES USEFUL AND HELP TIDY UP, I MAY BE LENIENT WITH YOU.

LENIENT?
I'LL TURN YOU INTO TOADS. BUT AT LEAST YOU'D BE SAFE FROM MY TABLE.

UNLESS I DECIDE TO HAVE A FRENCHMAN TO DINNER.

YOU'RE TOO KIND, SIR.
ARE YOU ALSO ORDINARY MEN DISPENSING ORDINARY JUSTICE?

FORGIVE MY RUDENESS.
THIS IS MISS ALICE CRISP, DAUGHTER OF WILLIAM CRISP, THE FOUNDER OF THE... LEAGUE OF ORDINARY GENTLEMEN, OR WHATEVER THEY WISH TO CALL IT.

HOW ENCHANTING.

IT'S A PLEASURE, MY DEAR.

MY NAME'S CRUMRIN.

ALOYSIUS CRUMRIN.

REALLY? ANY RELATION TO A MADAM LILLIAN CRUMRIN?
MY GRAND-MOTHER.

SHE ASKED TO BE REMEMBERED TO YOU.

OH.

GOOD HEAVENS, YOU KILLED HIM!
I DIDN'T EVEN SEE YOUR HAND MOVE.
I'M AFRAID SO. WARLOCKS AREN'T KNOWN FOR PLAYING FAIR.

IT'S A DEFINING TRAIT; MAGIC IS UNFAIR BY DEFINITION.

I THINK YOU'VE HUNG ONTO THIS LONG ENOUGH.

BESIDES, YOU SAW WHAT HAPPENED TO GOOSE FOR PLAYING FAIR.
THE KID'S GOT A POINT, MISS.

DON'T TAKE A KNIFE TO A GUNFIGHT, SIR?

HEH. GUESS I SHOULD HAVE TAKEN MY OWN ADVICE.

AS I TOOK MY LEAVE IN THE COMPANY OF THE SORCERER AND THE TALKING GOOSE, I FOUND MYSELF MUSING ON HOW ORDINARY IT ALL SEEMED. I WAS BEYOND TERROR OR WONDER, AND SIMPLY ACCEPTED IT, AS ONE ACCEPTS A DREAM.

HE'S *DEAD*.

THE MASTER IS *DEAD*.

YOU'RE FREE TO GO.
IT WASN'T HUMAN. IT WAS SOMETHING ELSE.

BUT SOMETHING IN ITS EYES SEEMED SOMEHOW FAMILIAR.

A LOOK OF WOUNDED DIGNITY I'D SEEN IN THE EYE OF MANY AN ORDINARY MAN.
GOODBYE, MISS CRISP.

WHERE ARE YOU GOING?
BACK TO HEADQUARTERS, OF COURSE, TO MAKE MY REPORT.

AND YOU'D BETTER START THINKING OF EXCUSES FOR YOUR ABSENCE THIS AFTERNOON.

I THOUGHT YOU WERE DONE WITH US.

OH, NO. I HAVE A FEW MORE LITTLE ERRANDS I'LL NEED YOUR HELP WITH. SEE YOU TOMORROW.

SO THIS... GOOSE BUSINESS. YOU DON'T SUPPOSE IT'LL JUST WEAR OFF, DO YOU?
I WAS PARALYZED, ADRIFT IN A SEA OF SECRETS AND CONSPIRACIES I COULDN'T BEGIN TO UNDERSTAND.
HE'D TWISTED SIMPLE RIGHT AND WRONG INTO A CORKSCREW.

I SUPPOSE THAT'S WHAT SORCERERS DO.

THERE WAS ONLY ONE WAY TO CLEAN UP THE MESS HE'D MADE OF MY MIND.

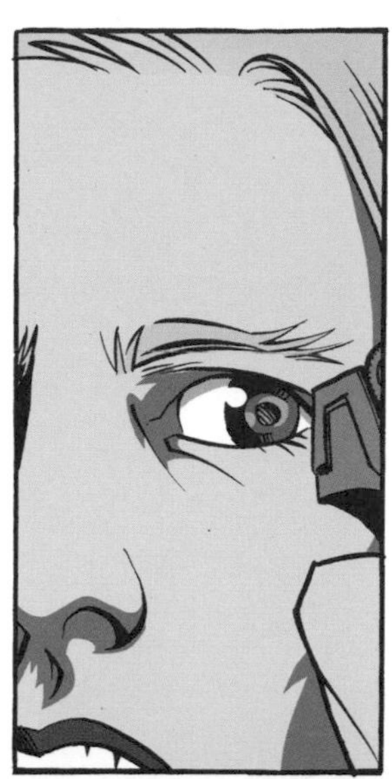

DAMN IT.

OW!
WHAT THE-

Chapter Two

LADY EMMA, INDEED. WE ALL KNOW SHE'S NO LADY.
WHO KNOWS WHERE SHE CAME FROM?

BUT THE CHAMPAGNE FLOWS LIKE WATER AROUND HERE. HARD TO ARGUE WITH THAT.
AND THE MONEY?

FOR ALL ANYONE KNOWS, SHE CONJURES IT OUT OF THIN AIR.
AND SPEAKING OF MAGIC, SHE USED TO GIVE HER AGE AS 40, AND NO ONE BELIEVED IT.

NOW, I'D GUESS 29. AND THAT'S BEING A BIT CATTY.
I'D KILL FOR HER SECRET.
COUNCILMAN GROSVENOR, YOU GORGEOUS MAN! SO LOVELY TO MEET YOU AT LAST. HOW GOES THE CAMPAIGN?

OVER. IT'S JUST MISTER GROSVENOR NOW, I'M AFRAID.
POOR DEAR. THAT'S WHAT YOU GET FOR CHAMPIONING THE COMMON MAN. THEY WON'T THANK YOU.

CHEER UP, OLD BOY. THERE ARE OTHER PATHS TO POWER THAN POLITICS.
AND WHO ARE THESE HANDSOME CREATURES?

LADY EMMA, MAY I PRESENT MY NIECE, ALICE CRISP, AND HER FIANCÉ–
WHAT SAY US GIRLS LEAVE THESE FUSTY MEN TO THEIR CIGARS AND GO POWDER OUR NOSES, EH?
ER, UH...

I SAY. I WASN'T EXPECTING *THAT*.
INTO A LADY'S PRIVATE BOUDOIR?
WE'D BETTER GO *AFTER* THEM.
IT'S NOT A *BOUDOIR*.

IT'S AN *ABATTOIR*.

HE'S A *HANDSOME* YOUNG MAN. WHEN IS THE DATE?
ARE YOU NERVOUS ABOUT YOUR *WEDDING NIGHT*? YOU CAN TELL AUNTIE EMMA.
OH, ER, WE *HAVEN'T*-
UH...

I KNOW I'M TERRIBLY OLD FASHIONED, BUT I STILL SAY A YOUNG COUPLE SHOULD WAIT.
WELL, OF COURSE-

I'M SO GLAD YOU FEEL THAT WAY.
GOOD HEAVENS! WHAT KIND OF POWDER ROOM IS THIS?

AREN'T YOU JUST DYING TO LEARN MY BEAUTY SECRETS?

I'M SURE I CAN GUESS A FEW. YOU'RE NOT THE ONLY ONE WHO'S BEEN TO KUMREINE...

...AUNT EMMA.

ALOYSIUS? MY GOODNESS, YOU'VE GROWN.

IN TEN YEARS, I HOPE SO.
BUT WHAT ARE YOU DOING HERE?
LOOKING UP MY FAVORITE AUNTY. IT'S SO STIFLING BACK HOME.

AND YOU WANT ME TO TAKE YOU IN, NO DOUBT?
AT LEAST I DIDN'T COME EMPTY-HANDED.

STAY AWAY FROM ME, BOTH OF YOU!
HOW THOUGHTFUL. SHE IS RATHER YOUNG AND FRESH.
SHE'S EXACTLY WHAT YOU NEED, AUNTY. TRUST ME.

STOP RIGHT THERE, SORCERESS!
I DON'T KNOW WHAT IT IS YOU INTEND, BUT I WON'T ALLOW-

TAKE YOUR WITHERED HAND OFF ME!
GACK!

OUR CHAPERONE WAS AN UNAVOIDABLE INCONVENIENCE, I FEAR.

FORGIVE ME.

I THINK NOT.
REMEMBER THE GAMES WE PLAYED WHEN YOU WERE A CHILD? MY ROCK BLUNTS YOUR SCISSORS.
WELL, YOUR LABORS ARE AT-
YOU SUPPOSE I HADN'T HEARD ABOUT OLD ELKAN? OR THE OTHERS? ALWAYS ABOUT HER WORK, EH BOY?
SHAME TO DESTROY SUCH A RARE MAGICAL HEIRLOOM. WHAT WOULD YOUR GRAND-MOTHER THINK?
BET YOU WISH YOU HAD AN EXTRA HAND ABOUT NOW.

BLAM

ARE YOU ALRIGHT?
HELP ME.

EXCELLENT WORK, SIR. YOU VANQUISHED HER.
GRACIOUS, SO MUCH POWER. SO MUCH...
INDEED.

ALAS, IT ALL COMES TO THE SAME END.

GOODBYE, AUNT EMMA.

IN THE MONTHS SINCE I LEARNED ALOYSIUS CRUMRIN'S TRUE NATURE, I HAVE BOTH HOPED AND FEARED THAT SOMEONE ELSE IN MY FATHER'S ANTI-SORCERY SOCIETY WOULD MAKE THE SAME DISCOVERY.
IT'S *FINISHED*. THE WITCH IS *DEAD*.

WELL *DONE*, FRED.
BUT FOR SUCH INTELLIGENT MEN, THEY'RE SURPRISINGLY UNOBSERVANT.

THESE TWO GAVE *CONSIDERABLE* AID.
I WOULDN'T HAVE TRUSTED MY DAUGHTER'S SAFETY TO *ANYONE ELSE*.
I SUPPOSE IT'S IN THE NATURE OF THE INCOMPETENT THAT THEY HAVE NOT THE WIT TO DETECT THEIR OWN FAILINGS.

YOU TWO GO DOWNSTAIRS AND SPRUCE THE PLACE UP. WE'LL BE DOWN DIRECTLY.

I SUPPOSE TONIGHT WENT EXACTLY ACCORDING TO PLAN, LIKE ALL THE OTHERS.
ON THE CONTRARY, IF IT WASN'T FOR YOU, MY GOOSE WOULD BE COOKED.

IS THIS ALL A GAME TO YOU? ARE WE JUST YOUR PAWNS, TO BE SACRIFICED WHEN IT'S CONVENIENT?
I ASSURE YOU, I'VE NEVER CONSIDERED ANYTHING MORE SERIOUS.

AND I'D SOONER DIE THAN SEE YOU COME TO HARM.

I WISH I COULD BELIEVE A WORD YOU SAID.

BETTER COOL THOSE LIPS, MISSY.
WHO THE DEVIL ARE YOU?

I'M THE DEVIL WITH THE GUN. I'D ADVISE YOU MIND YOUR MANNERS.
DON'T YOU READ THE NEWSPAPERS ANYMORE, ALICE?

SERGEANT JACKSON SMALLS, FORMERLY OF GOOSE DANIELS' PLATOON IN THE WAR.
DON'T KNOW HOW YOU RECOGNIZED ME.
RESPECTABLE PAPERS DON'T RUN STORIES OF THAT... COLOR.

I READ BETWEEN THE LINES.
SO WHERE IS GOOSE? HE'S BEEN MISSING FOR SIX MONTHS.

RIGHT HERE, SERGEANT. PUT THAT ROD AWAY.

ERR, HOW'S THE KATZEN-JAMMERS?
GOOSE.

DAMMIT, I TOLD YOU NOT TO GET INVOLVED WITH THESE LUNATICS.
AS GOOSE EXPLAINED THE SOCIETY'S PURPOSE AND HIS CURRENT PREDICAMENT TO JACKSON, I'M STRUCK AGAIN BY THE ABSURD JOKE OUR LIVES HAD BECOME.
HEH, I FIGURED IF I GOT IN TROUBLE, YOU'D BAIL ME OUT AGAIN.

WHAT'S THE MEANING OF THIS!?! WHO ARE YOU?

ONCE GOOSE EXPLAINED, FATHER LOST NO TIME RECRUITING OUR GUEST AS GOOSE'S REPLACEMENT.

IT'S ONLY UNTIL WE FIGURE OUT A WAY TO CURE CAPTAIN DANIELS.
AND WHEN'LL THAT HAPPEN?

WE'VE RUN INTO A BIT OF A PROBLEM.
I THINK I'VE FOUND THE RIGHT METHOD, BUT IT INVOLVES THE USE OF SORCERY.
I THOUGHT SORCERERS WERE BORN WITH THE ABILITY IN THEIR BLOOD.
IT SEEMS NOT. MY RESEARCH INDICATES THAT ANYONE CAN USE WITCHCRAFT, JUST AS ANYONE CAN SIN.

IF ANYONE WANTS MY OPINION, LEAVING ME LIKE THIS WOULD BE A MUCH BIGGER SIN.

STILL, I DON'T LIKE IT.
WELL I, FOR ONE, WON'T STAND IDLY BY, WILLIAM. IT'D BE UNGENTLEMANLY.

YOU'RE RIGHT, FRED. EVEN IF I DON'T TRUST MYSELF, I KNOW I CAN TRUST YOU.

I SAY, ENOUGH OF ALL THIS JAW. LET'S GET DOWN TO BUSINESS.
INDEED. DODSON AND I HAVE MADE A SIGNIFICANT DISCOVERY.

REALLY, PROFESSOR. IS THIS THE TIME?
YOU FORGET WHO TAUGHT YOU EVERYTHING YOU KNOW ABOUT THE OCCULT, MY LAD.

GENTLEMEN, I GIVE YOU...
HILLSBOROUGH.
A SEEMINGLY ORDINARY TOWN...

BUT WITH MORE WEALTH PER CAPITA THAN MADISON AVENUE. PROFESSOR PEABODY?

THIS IS THE MOTHERLODE OF EVIL, GENTLEMEN.
SURELY YOU EXAGGERATE, PEABODY.

DO I? WE TOOK A CLOSER LOOK INTO MS. EMMA ST. GRIEVE'S PAST, AS WELL AS THAT OF ELKEN GUNZT AND OUR OTHER TARGETS. IT WASN'T EASY.

CAN YOU IMAGINE WHAT WE FOUND?

GOOD LORD! CAN THIS BE TRUE?
HOW MANY CAME FROM THIS ONE LITTLE TOWN?

EVERY ONE OF THEM, GENTLEMEN.
EVERY ONE.

WE WERE DISPATCHED IN THE GUISE OF NEWLYWEDS WITH SERGEANT SMALLS AS OUR DRIVER.
HE'S PERSUASIVE, YOUR FATHER.
I'D PROMISED MYSELF I'D QUIT TAKING ORDERS AND BE MY OWN MAN.

DON'T WE ALL...
IT'D TAKEN TIME TO SORT THROUGH MY CONFUSION AND WORK OUT WHAT HAD HAPPENED TO ME.

WHY MY FEELINGS HAD SPUN SO OUT OF CONTROL, AND MY HEART WAS NO LONGER MY OWN.
SORCERY AGAIN.
AND I WAS POWERLESS TO RESIST IT.

IT DON'T LOOK LIKE THE HUB OF ALL EVIL.
AND HOW SHOULD SUCH A PLACE LOOK?

ANYWAY, ACCORDING TO PROFESSOR PEABODY, THERE'LL BE A MEETING PLACE WHERE SORCERERS GATHER TO PERFORM BLACK MAGIC.

LET'S TRY TO FIND IT.

I'D SAY THAT PLACE FITS THE BILL.
LOOKS LIKE MAGIC IS ALL THAT'S KEEPING IT FROM FALLING DOWN.
I'D PENETRATED MANY A DARK ABODE WITH ALOYSIUS. BUT THOUGH I COULDN'T SAY WHY, THIS ONE DISTURBED ME FAR MORE THAN ANY OTHER.

YOU TWO BETTER STAY NEAR THE *DOOR* WHILE I SWEEP FOR MAGICAL *TRAPS*.
WE OUGHT TO STICK *TOGETHER*.

LOOK, UNLIKELY AS IT SEEMS, YOUR FATHER PUT **ME** IN CHARGE. HE'S A **DECENT** MAN, BUT I DON'T WANT TO FIND OUT HOW FAR HIS DECENCY GOES IF YOU GET **KILLED** ON MY WATCH.

PLEASE?

SOMEHOW, I THINK DEATH TRAPS WOULD BE SAFER THAN *YOU*.
THERE ARE *NO* DEATH TRAPS HERE.
WHAT? HOW DO YOU *KNOW*?

BECAUSE IT'S MY *HOME*.

CAN I MAKE YOU SOME *COCOA*?

HMMM. HOPE I DON'T HAVE TO MEET YOU IN HERE, LADY.

SON OF A GUN.
DON'T YOU LOOK FAMILIAR...

YOU ENJOY MANIPULATING ME, DON'T YOU?
NOT AT ALL, BUT YOU'VE GIVEN ME LITTLE CHOICE.
BUT WHY A LOVE SPELL? THERE MUST HAVE BEEN OTHER METHODS.
NONE AS PLEASANT, TRUST ME.

HAH! TRUST YOU?
WHY NOT? I'VE BEEN DOING EXACTLY WHAT YOUR FATHER WANTS.

RIDDING THE WORLD OF DANGEROUS SORCERERS.
ISN'T THAT WHAT YOU ALL WANTED?
ARE YOU SURE THIS ISN'T GOING TO HURT?
I HONESTLY HAVE NO IDEA.
WAIT, WHAT?

WHEW, THAT WAS EASIER THAN I THOUGHT.
INDEED.

LET'S SEE WHAT THIS NEXT ONE DOES.

TAKE A BREAK, LOVEBIRDS. THERE'S SOMETHING YOU BOTH SHOULD SEE.
IS IT SAFE?

IN A PLACE LIKE THIS? DO YOU HAVE TO ASK?
BUT I THINK I KNOW A WAY TO MAKE IT A BIT SAFER.

HANDS WHERE I CAN SEE 'EM, KID. YOU GOT SOME EXPLAINING TO DO.

HSSSSS

GAH!
I SUPPOSE I DO. PLEASE FORGIVE MY MANNERS. THIS IS NO WAY TO TREAT A GUEST IN ONE'S HOME.

FOOOOSH

I ASSURE YOU I MEAN NO HARM TO YOU OR MISS CRISP.

WHY DON'T WE JUST POUR SOME TEA AND DISCUSS IT?
BEFORE SOMEONE GETS HURT.
BANG
AAAAAAAAAAAAAHHHH!!!

GOOD LORD!
RUN!

WHAT HAVE I DONE!?!
WHAT HAVE I DONE!?!

DON'T YOU GET IT, MISS? HE WAS ONE OF THEM!
I KNOW. I'VE KNOWN FOR MONTHS. HE CAST A... A SPELL ON ME...
GOOD RIDDANCE, THEN.

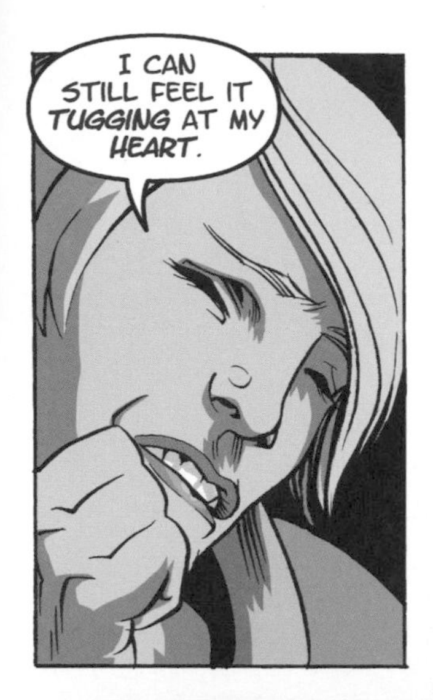
I CAN STILL FEEL IT TUGGING AT MY HEART.

WE'LL GO BACK TO THE OLD MEN.
LET'S HOPE THEY'LL KNOW WHAT TO DO ABOUT THIS.

HELLO... GRANDMOTHER.

AH, SMALLS. REPORT! WHERE'S ALOYSIUS?

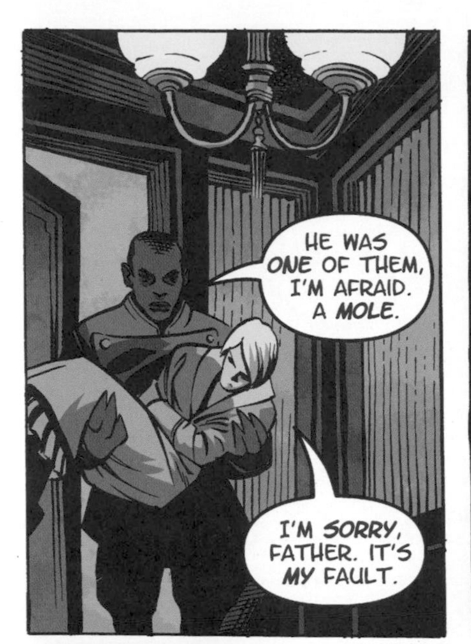
HE WAS ONE OF THEM, I'M AFRAID. A MOLE.
I'M SORRY, FATHER. IT'S MY FAULT.

THE DEUCE YOU SAY! DID YOU DISPATCH HIM?

ACTUALLY, IT WAS MISS CRISP HERE. NERVES OF STEEL, THIS ONE.

FATHER? ARE YOU ALRIGHT?
GOOD! WE'LL SOON SORT OUT THE REST OF THEM.

SHE'S HAD A TRYING TIME, THOUGH. WE BOTH HAVE. I'LL MAKE A FULL REPORT WHEN I'VE-

KRAK

JACKSON!

IT'S ASTONISHINGLY SIMPLE, MAGIC.
I'M FRANKLY AMAZED NO ONE HAS USED IT TO CONQUER THE WORLD.

PEOPLE SIMPLY HAVE NO VISION. I'LL BE RUNNING THIS COUNTRY BEFORE THE YEAR IS OUT.

AND THE BEST PART IS THAT THOSE SORCERERS IN HILLSBOROUGH WON'T EVEN SEE ME COMING.

ALICE, RUN! GET HELP!

HONESTLY, YOU WAR HEROES AND YOUR THEATRICS.

AS IF THERE'S ANY HELP TO FIND.
I KNOW NOW WHAT EVE HAD FELT WHEN SHE TASTED THE APPLE.

WHATEVER I OR MY FATHER HAD TOLD OURSELVES, THAT WE WERE DECENT FOLK FIGHTING FOR THE GREATER GOOD...

WE REALLY JUST WANTED TO SEE MAGIC.
IT SEDUCED US ALL. THE MORE WE FOUGHT IT, THE MORE IT WRAPPED ITS TERRIBLE INFLUENCE AROUND US, EATING AWAY OUR BETTER NATURES...

UNTIL WE COULDN'T SEE ANYTHING ELSE.
HELLO? ALOYSIUS?

UNTIL IT BECAME MY ONLY HOPE.
OH, LORD.
AYE, IT'S A SHAME, REALLY. I LOVED THAT RUG.

WHO'S THERE!?!
JUST A TIRED OLD WOMAN, DEAR. DO SIT DOWN.

ARE YOU A WITCH?
MOST CERTAINLY.
BUT I ASSURE YOU, I SHALL NEITHER TURN YOU INTO A TOAD NOR BATHE IN YOUR BLOOD.
WHY NOT?

JUST BECAUSE I'M A WITCH DON'T MEAN I AIN'T A GOOD CHRISTIAN.

BESIDES, ME GRANDSON THINKS THE *WORLD* OF YOU. I WOULDN'T WANT TO *UPSET* HIM.
YOUR GRANDSON?
ALOYSIUS. ACTUALLY, HE'S ME GREAT, *GREAT* GRANDSON.

I WERE THE *FIRST* WITCH IN *HILLSBOROUGH*, YOU SEE.

WE LIVED IN A LITTLE VALLEY ON THE *GREEN ISLE*, USING OUR *CRAFT* TO LOOK AFTER THE LOCAL *VILLAGERS*.
ONE DAY, THE MEN IN BLACK CAME TO *BURN* US.

THEY *CLAIMED* TO BE CHRISTIAN *SOLDIERS*. BUT *LITTLE* DID THEY RESEMBLE THE CHRISTIANS *WE* KNEW.
THEIRS WAS A *HATEFUL* GOD.

THEY CAUGHT ME GRANDMOTHER HELPING A RUNAWAY GIRL GIVE BIRTH.

I ESCAPED BY PATHS UNKNOWN TO MOST MORTALS...

...AND FOUND A PLACE NO MORTAL HAD EVER TROD.

I FOUND PEACE THERE.
BUT IT WEREN'T TO LAST.

YET, THEY ONLY WANTED WHAT I'D WANTED, TO BE LEFT IN PEACE. I PITIED THEM.

AND I NEEDED COMPANY. FOR ALL MY FEAR AND DISTRUST OF HUMANITY...

...I WAS HUMAN TOO.

THEY WERE DECENT ENOUGH. I HELPED THEM THROUGH THAT FIRST WINTER, AND THEN THE NEXT. I BECAME THEIR WITCH.

EVENTUALLY, A FEW WIVES AND DAUGHTERS CAME TO ME TO LEARN THE CRAFT.
I TAUGHT THEM TO CALM THE WINDS, TO SUMMON RAIN, TO ENTICE THE SUN...

...AND OTHER SECRETS ONLY WITCHES KNOW. THE LITTLE TOWN PROSPERED.

NATURALLY, THEIR HUSBANDS RECKONED THEY COULD USE THE CRAFT TO BECOME POWERFUL MEN.

SOMETHING I STRICTLY FORBADE.

I KNEW ALL TOO WELL THE TEMPTATIONS OF WITCHCRAFT, AND HOW THEY COULD BRING DOWN THE STORM OF HATRED UPON US.
THE MEN IN BLACK WERE STILL OUT THERE.

LIKE YOUR FATHER.
I DON'T UNDERSTAND.

IF YOU FORBADE IT, WHY ARE ALL THESE SORCERERS RUNNING AROUND THE COUNTRY DOING WHATEVER THEY PLEASE?

I'M AFRAID I LOST ME POWER TO DISSUADE THEM.
OH? HOW SO?

I DIED, YOU SEE.

I SHOULD HAVE SCREAMED AND RUN FROM THE ROOM. I SHOULD HAVE BEEN SURPRISED.
BUT I THINK I'D KNOWN FROM THE MOMENT I SAT DOWN.

I JUST FOLLOWED THE GHOST WOMAN UPSTAIRS.
OF THE LIVING DESCENDANTS OF ME LITTLE TOWN, ONLY ME POOR GRANDSON SEES THE NEED TO PUT A STOP TO THESE WICKED WITCHES AND WARLOCKS.
NOTHING SURPRISED ME NOW. HORRORS WERE COMMONPLACE. MY WORLD HAD SHIFTED.
I GAVE THEM EVERYTHING, THINKING IT WOULD APPEASE THEIR WANTING.
I SUPPOSE MAGIC HAS A WAY OF TURNING PEOPLE BAD.
EVEN ALOYSIUS.

WHAT DO YOU MEAN?
THE WAY HE USED MY FATHER AND GOOSE DANIELS. AND WHEN I LEARNED HIS SECRET, HE CAST A LOVE SPELL ON ME...

HE WHAT?
DON'T BE ABSURD, YOUNG LADY. LOVE SPELL INDEED!

THERE'S NO SUCH THING AS LOVE SPELLS?
ON THE CONTRARY, THERE ARE DOZENS.

BUT ME GRANDSON WOULDN'T DREAM OF USING ONE.
HE'S A GENTLEMEN.
YOU'RE JUST A FOOLISH WOMAN THAT DON'T KNOW YOUR OWN HEART.

IT'S HIS HEART THAT'S WOUNDED.
ALAS, I CAN'T HELP HIM.

ONLY A LIVING HAND CAN CAST SUCH A SPELL.

AND I THINK I KNEW THAT THIS, TOO, WAS INEVITABLE. MAGIC ISN'T A TOOL FOR WITCHES.
THEY'RE THE TOOLS.

WE DON'T USE IT, IT USES US.
IS THAT THE NEW CAMPAIGN POSTER?

PERFECT.
I WANT TEN THOUSAND PRINTED BY MORNING.
MAGIC
CRISP
STATE SENATE

AND SEND SOMEONE 'ROUND TO THE TIMES. I WANT A REPORTER HERE BY 8:00 AM.

I'M GOING TO MAKE ALL YOUR DREAMS COME TRUE, WILLIAM. THE COMMON FOLK UNITED UNDER YOUR BENEVOLENT LEADERSHIP. AREN'T YOU PLEASED?

ARE YOU SURE YOU'RE STRONG ENOUGH? YOU LOOKED PRETTY BAD AN HOUR AGO.

DOES IT MATTER? EVEN IF I WERE DYING ON MY FEET, I'D STILL HAVE A JOB TO DO.
WHY DO YOU CARE WHAT HAPPENS TO MY FATHER AND THE REST OF THEM?

I CARE WHAT HAPPENS TO YOU.

WHY?
ISN'T IT OBVIOUS?
NOT REALLY.

BECAUSE YOU'RE THE MOST HARDHEADED, STUBBORN, MADDENING, EXTRAORDINARY WOMAN I'VE EVER MET.

EXCEPTING MY GRANDMOTHER, OF COURSE.

IS THAT WHY YOU MADE UP THAT LOVE SPELL STORY?
YOU DID THAT, AS I RECALL.
BUT I WASN'T ABOUT TO CONTRADICT A LADY.

AND I SUPPOSE IT MADE IT EASIER TO CONTROL ME.
I NEVER NEEDED TO.

WE BOTH WANTED THE SAME THINGS.
TO BELIEVE WE STILL DO.
FOR HEAVEN'S SAKE, ALOYSIUS!

IS THIS REALLY THE APPROPRIATE MOMENT?

QUITE RIGHT. MY APOLOGIES.

I COULDN'T DECIDE WHICH WOULD BE WORSE...
THEY SAY YOU SHOULD HOPE FOR NOTHING MORE THAN JOBS AND FOOD ON THE TABLE!
MAGIC
CRISP
A JOB IS DIGNITY

WHETHER THE CROWD WAS ENCHANTED...
I SAY, DEMAND MORE!
DEMAND MAGIC!
WE WANT JOBS
FA CAT GO HOM
NEW DEAL NOW!
OR IF THEY WERE REALLY SWALLOWING THIS GARBAGE.

MAGIC IS WHAT I OFFER, GENTLEMEN!
DON'T BELIEVE ME?

BELIEVE THIS! H.W. CRISP DOESN'T JUST PROMISE MAGIC!
HE DELIVERS!

IT'S ASTONISHING HOW MUCH EASIER THIS PROCESS IS WHEN THE NEWSPAPERS WRITE WHAT YOU WANT THEM TO.
I'LL WAGER I'M NOT THE FIRST TO DISCOVER THIS.
YOU CAN'T RULE THE WORLD BY MAGIC.

YOU'VE NO CONCEPT OF THE DANGER.

YOU'LL FORGIVE ME IF I DON'T TAKE YOUR WORD FOR IT.
BESIDES, WHO'S GOING TO STOP ME. YOU?

LOOK AROUND! I'VE ALREADY ACQUIRED AN ARMY.
ANY ONE OF THEM WOULD DEFEND ME TO THE DEATH.
WILL YOU FIGHT THEM ALL?

I DON'T HAVE TO.
SNAP

WHAT THE HELL'S GOING ON?
YOUCH! SOMEONE GET THE NUMBER O' THAT TRUCK.
A WISE YOUNG WOMAN ONCE TOLD ME...

...THAT THE TRAGEDY OF A FOOL IS THAT HIS FOOLISHNESS RENDERS HIM INCAPABLE OF SEEING WHAT A FOOL HE IS.
OR SOMETHING TO THAT-

YOU! WHY, I OUGHTTA-
JACKSON, STOP!

HE'S NOT THE ONE YOU NEED TO PUMMEL.
SHE'S RIGHT. IT'S GROSVENOR.

SO ALOYSIUS IS A SORCERER, BUT GROSVENOR IS THE BAD GUY?
WAIT, WHAT? THE KID'S A SORCERER?
JEEZ, GOOSE. TRY TO KEEP UP.
HEY, I SPENT THE LAST SIX MONTHS LAYING EGGS AND HOPING NO ONE WOULD GET HUNGRY ENOUGH TO EAT ME-
THE THORT NEVER LEFT ME MIND THAT 'OLE TIME, LADDIE.

INTERESTING CREATURE, ISN'T HE? ONCE YOU'VE ENSNARED HIM, HE IS YOUR BOUND SERVANT FOREVER.
NOTHING CAN LIFT THE ENCHANTMENT.

YER A BIT BIG NOW, BUT I ET BIGGER.
STOP!

OOF!
KROVCH

SOMETHING EVERY SORCERER IN HILLSBOROUGH LEARNS AT THEIR MOTHER'S KNEE.
BUTTERWORM, GO HOME.

YOU'RE A CHILD PLAYING WITH YOUR FATHER'S GUN, SIR. PUT IT DOWN AND COME AWAY.

FRED GROSVENOR, YOU HAVE SOME SERIOUS EXPLAINING TO DO.

THIS IS MY FATHER'S GUN, SORCERER. DON'T TRY ANYTHING.
FRED, WHAT IN HEAVEN'S NAME IS THIS?

I'M SORRY, WILL. THE POWER WAS JUST TOO TEMPTING.

WHEN WILL YOU LEARN?
FZZZ

OH, I'M LEARNING MORE ALL THE TIME.
ZZZZT

I KNEW SORCERERS WOULD COME FOR ME EVENTUALLY, SO I CAST A SPELL OF PROTECTION.

WITHIN THIS CHAMBER, NO MAGIC CAN HARM ME.
AND NOW, I SHALL CARRY OUT THE COVENANT THAT BROUGHT US ALL TOGETHER.
THE SORCERER MUST DIE!

ESCARIOT!

I TRUSTED YOU WITH EVERYTHING! MY SECRETS! MY DAUGHTER'S LIFE!
BLAM

FATHER! NO-!

GENTLEMEN, IF I CAN SHOOT MY BEST FRIEND DOWN, PLEASE BELIEVE I WON'T HESITATE SHOOT YOU BOTH IF YOU COME ANY NEARER.

CAN YOU DO ANYTHING?
IT'S TOO LATE.

MR. SMALLS, TAKE CARE OF HER. I'LL ATTEND TO MR. GROSVENOR.
WHAT ARE YOU GOING TO DO?

HE'S A ROGUE SORCERER. THERE'S ONLY ONE WAY TO STOP HIM.

SO, HOW GOES YER FIRST DAY AS A WARLOCK, EH?

WERE IT EVERYTHING YEH HOPED FOR?

YER SPELLWORK COULD USE SOME REFININ'. YEH WERE SUPPOSED TO FEED ME.

JUST A WEE BITTY OVERSIGHT!

SHOULDN'T WE HELP HIM?

NO. HE'S BEYOND HELPING NOW.

I THOUGHT I'D SEEN THE LAST OF ALOYSIUS CRUMRIN, BUT HE WAS NOTHING IF NOT PERSISTANT.

I SUPPOSE YOU'VE COME TO TAKE ME AWAY.
IS THAT WHAT YOU WANT?
DOES IT MATTER?

I DON'T KNOW IF WHAT I FEEL IN MY HEART IS TRUE...
BUT I NO LONGER HAVE THE STRENGTH TO RESIST.

DO WITH ME WHAT YOU LIKE.
YOU'VE WON.
VERY WELL.

GOODBYE, ALICE CRISP.

AND THEN EVERYTHING WENT-

HELLO, GRANDMOTHER. I THOUGHT YOU'D WANT THESE *BACK*.

YOU MAY NOT NEED THEM WHERE *YOU* ARE...

BUT THEY DON'T BELONG IN *THIS* WORLD ANYMORE.

EXCUSE ME.

DO YOU KNOW A GOOD HOTEL AROUND HERE?
OH, HELLO. YES, THERE'S ONE UP THE ROAD AT THE TOWN SQUARE.

WILL THEY ACCOMMODATE US, DO YOU THINK? SOME HOTELS CAN BE TOUCHY ABOUT...

...CERTAIN THINGS.

YOU'LL BE FINE. THIS TOWN IS KIND TO PEOPLE WHO'RE A BIT...
...DIFFERENT.

YOU SEEM STRANGELY FAMILIAR. HAVE WE MET?

I THINK I WOULD HAVE REMEMBERED.
THE END

A FEW MORE WORDS ABOUT CHILDREN, NIGHTMARES, AND OUTCASTS

Every story has a beginning, and that's always exciting. It is a wonderful and special thing to be there for the beginning of someone's story, to watch them go out into the world and into other people's lives. You have no idea what the middle will be like, or how it will end. That's the definition of adventure.

But every story has an end, and that's always at least a little bit sad. When you love the people in the story, you don't want to turn that last page. It takes some courage to face the prospect of saying goodbye. The more you love them, the braver you have to be.

When Max entered my life, so did fear. They don't tell you that in stories. In books, if people have a baby, it's part of the happy ending, never at the beginning of the adventure.

Up until that point, I had mostly stridden through life in big stompy boots, up to my knees in adventure. I moved to the big city; made all sorts — and I do mean all sorts — of friends, mostly through Craigslist; dressed up in crazy costumes and went dancing and walked home just before dawn through sketchy neighborhoods. I shaved my head and rode motorcycles and went to Burning Man. I traveled to several interesting countries, although not as many as I wanted, and never for long enough. I practiced martial arts and fantasized about someone trying to attack me just so I could prove what a big, bad person I was.

Seldom did I ask myself, "Is this safe?" And if I did, "Oh, probably," was good enough. I made it through healthy and whole due more to luck and being a good judge of character than anything else. I learned a lot about the world and myself. Adventure is good for that. I had many chances to decide who I wanted to be, just like a choose-your-own-way book, except you can't turn the page back and try again. Each decision you make shapes who you are and what happens years later in ways you can't possibly predict.

Eventually, I wondered if there might be another kind of adventure that was worth having, and I had Max.

Then, suddenly, I was afraid.

First I was afraid he would stop breathing in the middle of the night, that the little spark that animates him would just quietly go out without warning, and I'd never see his sweet smile again. I had only known him for a few hours, but I knew that I couldn't live in a world without him in it, and that I would love him for the rest of my life. I knew that I would die to protect him without a second thought, with a smile, if I could just know he'd be safe.

When he began crawling and hitting his head, I felt like I should make him wear a helmet at all times until age 10 just to stop worrying. I became incapable of hearing or reading stories about any kind of child abuse. Maybe more than anything, I fear knowing that there will be a last time I see his face, a last time I'll hold him, a last time I'll hear him laugh. Every story has an end.

Both fortunately and unfortunately, Max is a lot like me so far. He's an adventurer. A baby of action, intent on finding out what's behind the locked cabinet door and whether he can climb over the back of the sofa. Answer: Yes. He goes over and through obstacles rather than around them. And he trusts people. Strangers. Everybody. No fear whatsoever. Adventure is his destiny.

In life, love is the true key to adventure, and the real test of courage. Max taught me that. Until you have someone you love, whom you can't imagine living in a world without, you can't really know whether you're brave. Adventures can do worse than make you late for dinner.

When you're responsible for someone, that's when you find out who you are and what you're capable of. When you love someone — that's when the real adventure begins.

–Kelly Crumrin, Fall 2014

As a child in Illinois, Kelly Crumrin enjoyed picking up snakes, but was terrified of tent caterpillars, which she tried to set on fire. Somehow she survived long enough to move to the San Francisco Bay Area and become a writer.

Courtney Crumrin

Volume Seven

Tales of a Warlock

Cover Gallery

Cover artwork for *Courtney Crumrin Tales: A Portrait of a Young Warlock*.

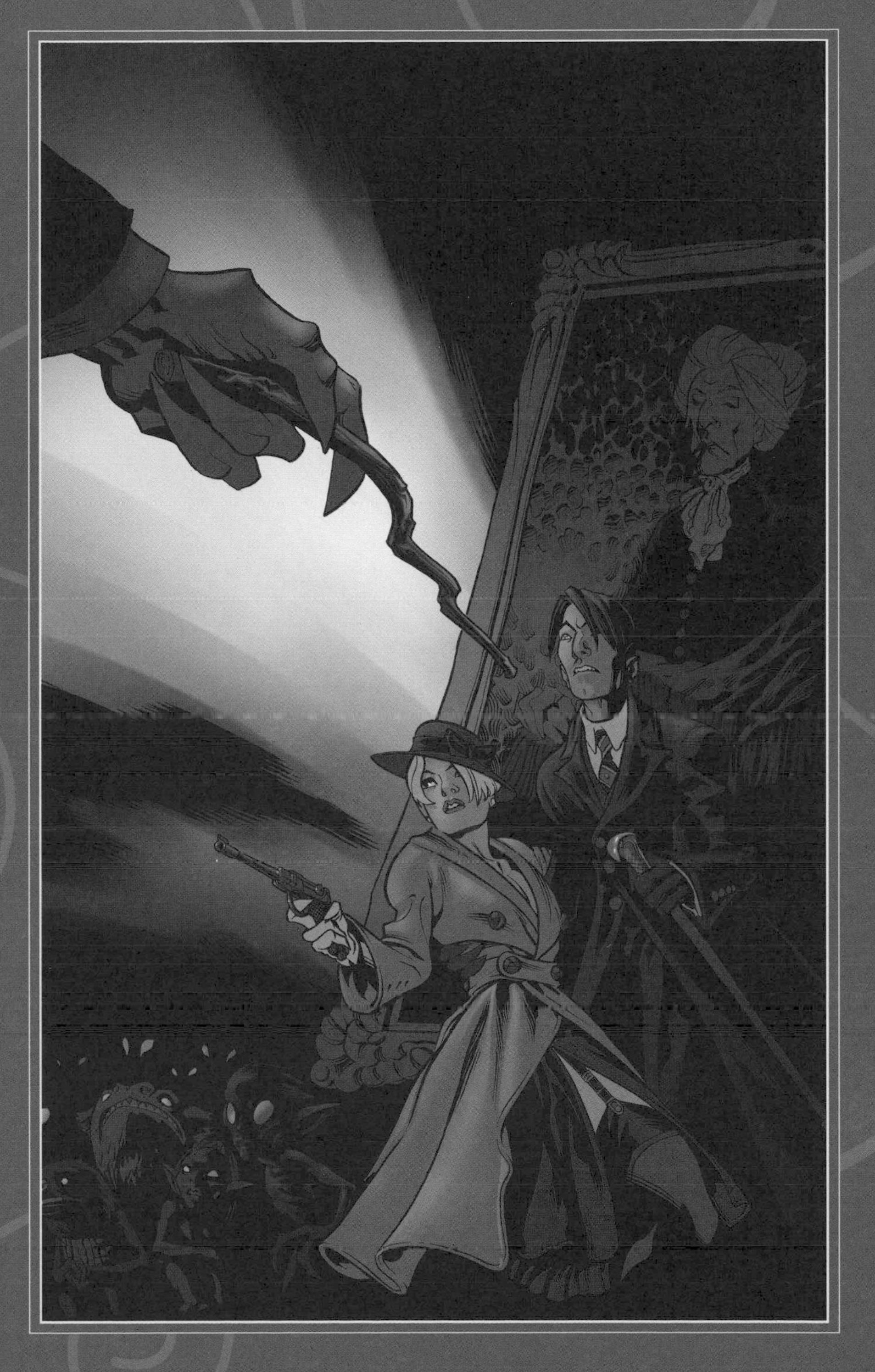

Cover artwork for *Courtney Crumrin Tales: The League of Ordinary Gentlemen.*

Art from an unused flyer for the original series.

Early sketches of Aloysius Crumrin in his later years.

A Christmas pinup of Aloysius and Courtney.

A t-shirt design which was also used as a wine label.

A commission of Aloysius Crumrin.

Ted Naifeh

Ted Naifeh first appeared in the independent comics scene in 1999 as the artist for *Gloomcookie*, co-created with Serena Valentino. After a successful run, Ted decided to strike out on his own, writing and drawing *Courtney Crumrin and the Night Things*, a spooky middle-grade series about a grumpy little girl and her adventures with her warlock uncle.

Nominated for an Eisner Award for best limited series, *Courtney Crumrin's* success paved the way for *Polly and the Pirates*, about a prim and proper girl kidnapped by pirates convinced she was the daughter of their long-lost queen.

Over the next few years, Ted wrote four volumes of *Courtney Crumrin*, plus a spin-off book about her uncle. He also co-created *How Loathsome* with Tristan Crane, and illustrated two volumes of *Death Junior* with screenwriter Gary Whitta. For bestselling author Holly Black, he illustrated *The Good Neighbors*, a three-volume graphic novel series published by Scholastic.

Over the last decade, Ted wrote the sequel to *Polly and the Pirates*, illustrated by *Spider-Gwen* artist Robbi Rodriquez. To celebrate the 10th anniversary of *Courtney Crumrin*, he wrote and illustrated the final two volumes of the series. He followed that up with a new teen heroine, *Princess Ugg*, a barbarian girl going to Princess Finishing School.

Branching out into more experimental projects, Ted wrote and illustrated *Night's Dominion*, a genre-mash-up of superheroes and fantasy. He also wrote *Kriss*, a dark hero's journey illustrated by Warren Wucinich, about a young heir to a fallen kingdom, whose destiny to restore his birthright may be a fate worse than death.

Ted is currently writing Volume 2 of *Kriss*, and a new book for Abrams called *Witch For Hire*, about a problem solving teen who's never seen without her pointy hat.

Ted lives in San Francisco, because he likes dreary weather.